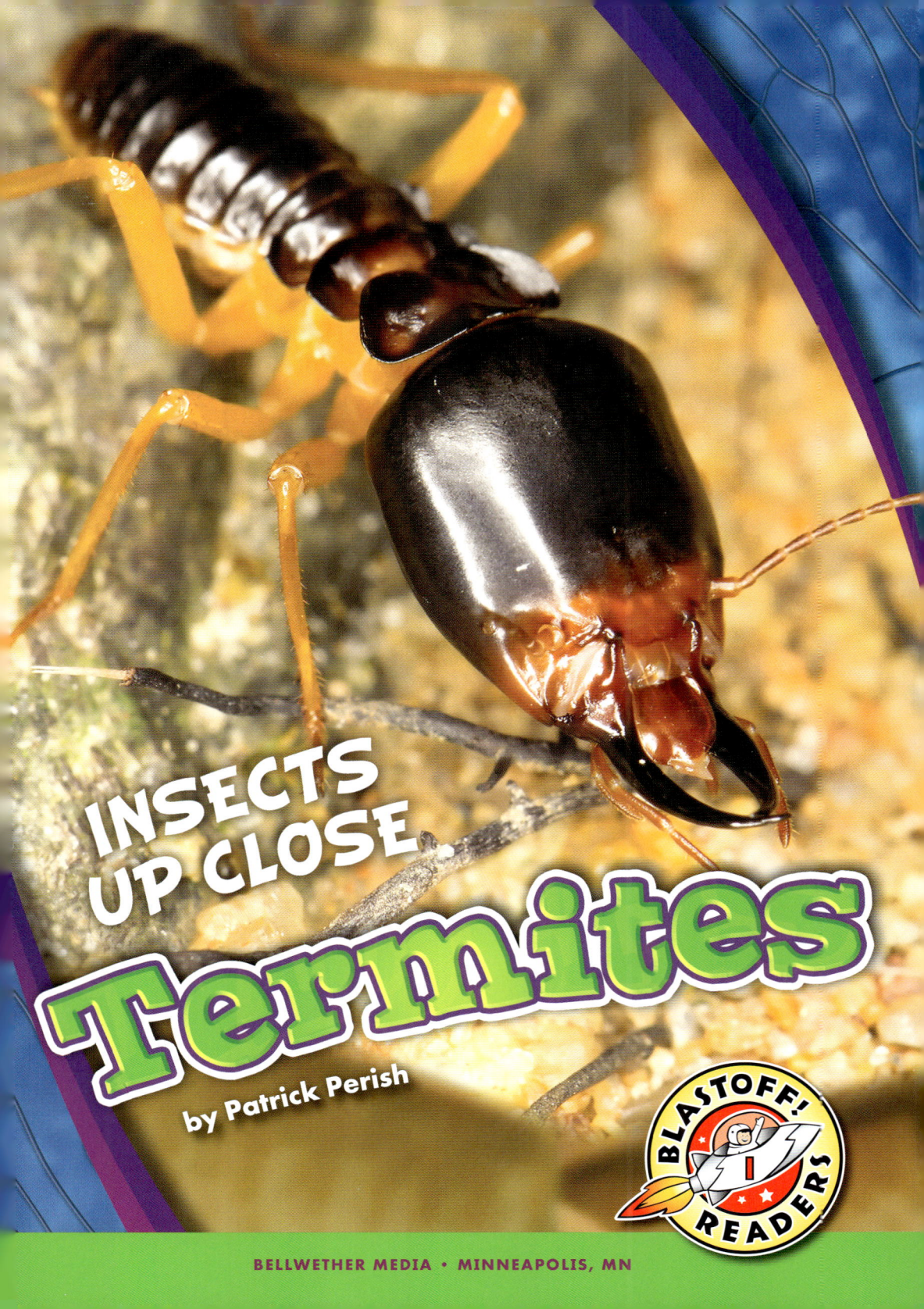

INSECTS UP CLOSE

Termites

by Patrick Perish

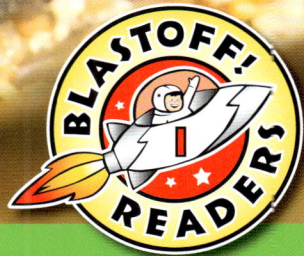

BELLWETHER MEDIA • MINNEAPOLIS, MN

Note to Librarians, Teachers, and Parents:

Blastoff! Readers are carefully developed by literacy experts and combine standards-based content with developmentally appropriate text.

Level 1 provides the most support through repetition of high-frequency words, light text, predictable sentence patterns, and strong visual support.

Level 2 offers early readers a bit more challenge through varied simple sentences, increased text load, and less repetition of high-frequency words.

Level 3 advances early-fluent readers toward fluency through increased text and concept load, less reliance on visuals, longer sentences, and more literary language.

Level 4 builds reading stamina by providing more text per page, increased use of punctuation, greater variation in sentence patterns, and increasingly challenging vocabulary.

Level 5 encourages children to move from "learning to read" to "reading to learn" by providing even more text, varied writing styles, and less familiar topics.

Whichever book is right for your reader, Blastoff! Readers are the perfect books to build confidence and encourage a love of reading that will last a lifetime!

This edition first published in 2018 by Bellwether Media, Inc.

No part of this publication may be reproduced in whole or in part without written permission of the publisher. For information regarding permission, write to Bellwether Media, Inc., Attention: Permissions Department, 5357 Penn Avenue South, Minneapolis, MN 55419.

Library of Congress Cataloging-in-Publication Data

Names: Perish, Patrick, author.
Title: Termites / by Patrick Perish.
Description: Minneapolis, MN : Bellwether Media, Inc., 2018. | Series: Blastoff! Readers. Insects Up Close |
    Audience: Age 5-8. | Audience: K to Grade 3. | Includes bibliographical references and index.
Identifiers: LCCN 2017028790| ISBN 9781626177192 (hardcover) | ISBN 9781681034126 (ebook)
Subjects: LCSH: Termites–Juvenile literature.
Classification: LCC QL529 .P47 2018 | DDC 595.7/36–dc23
LC record available at https://lccn.loc.gov/2017028790

Editor: Nathan Sommer   Designer: Steve Porter

Printed in the United States of America, North Mankato, MN.

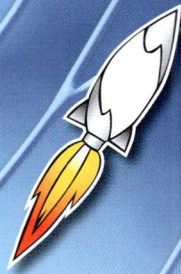

Table of Contents

What Are Termites?

Termites love to eat wood. They live together in big **colonies**.

colony

Each termite has a job. **Soldier** termites guard the colony with sharp **pincers**.

soldier termites

pincers

Worker termites are small and **pale**. They build the colony's nest.

worker termites

ACTUAL SIZE:
worker termite

9

Queen termites
are very big.
They lay eggs
all day long.

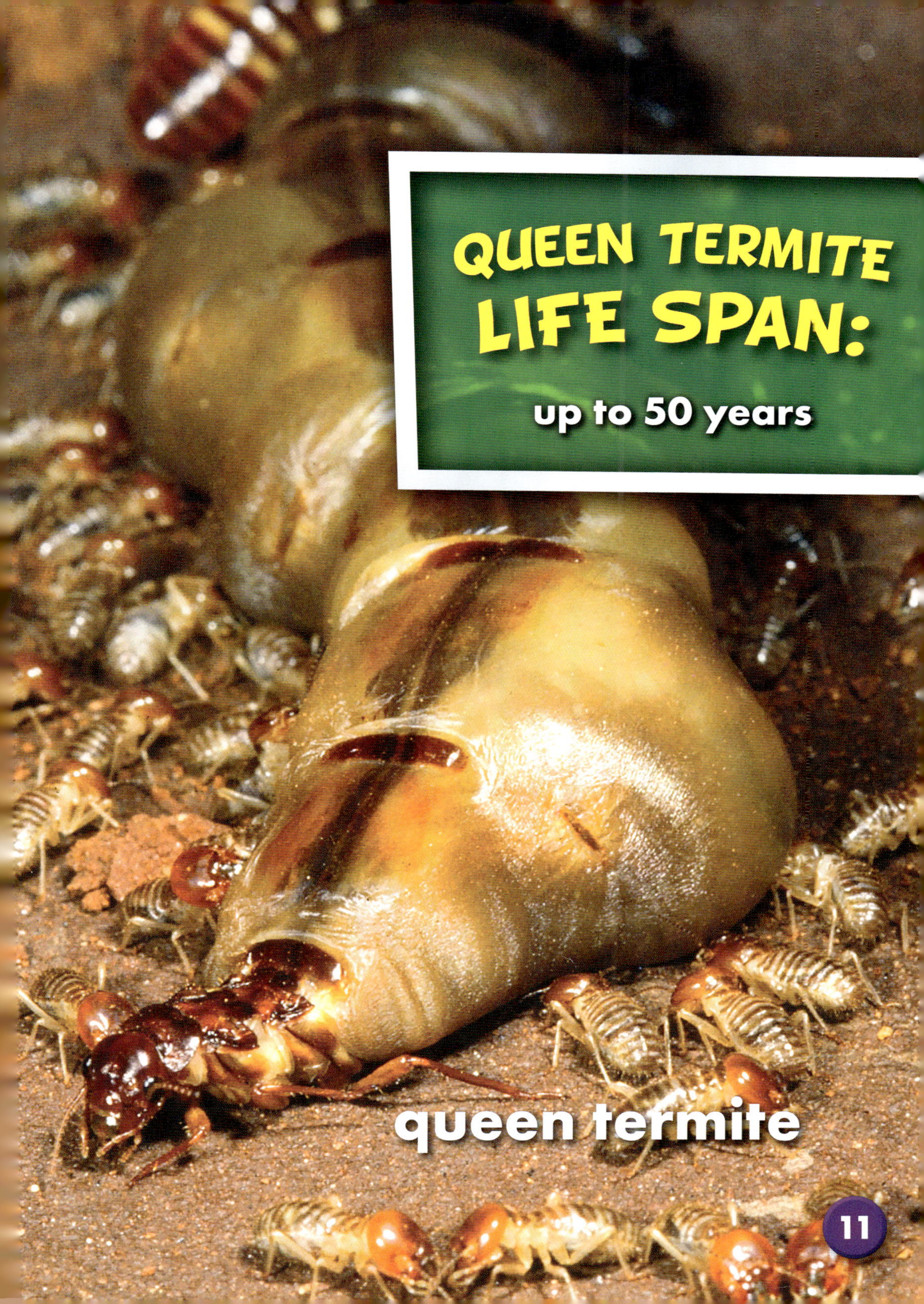

QUEEN TERMITE LIFE SPAN:

up to 50 years

queen termite

Life in the Nest

Termites eat wood and plants. They live in dark, wet nests.

termite nest

FAVORITE FOOD:

wood

Termites build nests in trees or out of earth. Some nests are taller than people!

termite nest

15

Growing Up

Queen and king termites fly to find one another. Then they lose their wings and start colonies.

wings

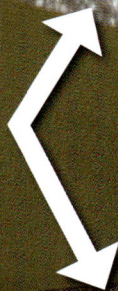

Queens lay millions of eggs each year. **Nymphs** soon **hatch** and take on different jobs.

eggs

nymphs

Swarmer termites grow wings. They fly off to start their own colonies!

swarmer
termites

Glossary

colonies

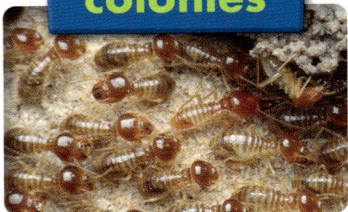

groups of termites that work together to live

pale

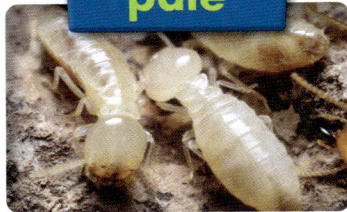

light in color or having little color

hatch

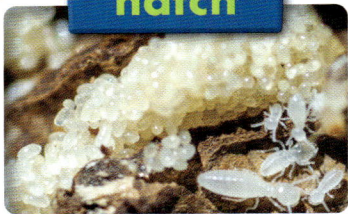

to break out of an egg

pincers

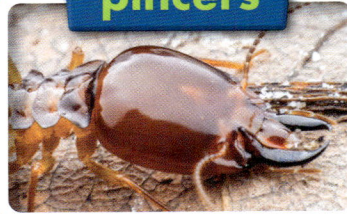

hooks at the end of a soldier termite's body used for fighting enemies

nymphs

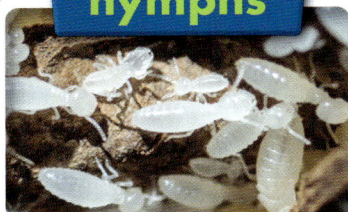

young insects; nymphs look like small adults without full wings.

soldier

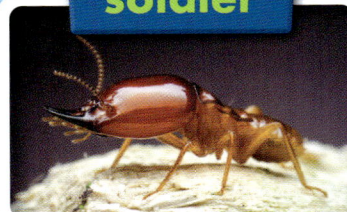

an insect that fights or defends against other insects

To Learn More

AT THE LIBRARY

Bodden, Valerie. *Termites*. Mankato, Minn.: Creative Paperbacks, 2014.

Porter, Esther. *Termites*. North Mankato, Minn.: Capstone Press, 2014.

Schuh, Mari. *Termites*. Minneapolis, Minn.: Bullfrog Books, 2015.

ON THE WEB

Learning more about termites is as easy as 1, 2, 3.

1. Go to www.factsurfer.com.

2. Enter "termites" into the search box.

3. Click the "Surf" button and you will see a list of related web sites.

With factsurfer.com, finding more information is just a click away.

Index

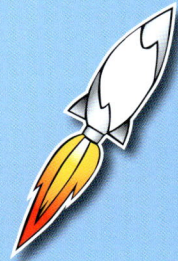